Gay Haiku

GAY HAIKU

Joel Derfner

Broadway Books
New York

For information, address Broadway Books, a division of Random House, Inc.

PRINTED IN THE UNITED STATES OF AMERICA

Visit our Web site at www.broadwaybooks.com

First edition published June 2005

Library of Congress Cataloging-in-Publication Data

Derfner, Joel.

Gay haiku / Joel Derfner.—1st ed.

p. cm.

1. Gay men—Poetry. 2. Haiku, American. I. Title.

PS3604.E754G39 2005

811'.6—dc22 2004056975

ISBN 0-7679-1984-X

10 9 8 7 6 5 4 3 2 1

For Mark Gray

Foreword

This book happened because of a bad breakup.

I suspect most books happen because of a bad breakup; one could make a case, I suppose, against *The History of the Decline and Fall of the Roman Empire,* but secretly I think Gibbon had heartbreak on the brain when he started writing.

Anyway, it was winter of 2002. My ex had moved out, taking with him the hideous couch (thank God) but leaving the dog (thank God) and a four-hundred-dollar bill for phone calls to his new boyfriend in Canada (because he couldn't have the decency to wait until he'd left to start seeing somebody else, oh, no),

and I was alone—well, I had the dog—in our vast three-bedroom apartment in the middle of nowhere in Washington Heights. Having learned just how spectacularly disastrous relationships could be from my old boyfriend, I set out instantly to find a new one.

I went on date after date after date, each one worse than the last.

Take, for example, the guy I'll call James (mostly because that's his name). We had a great lunch at which we flirted delightfully for two hours; then we decided we wanted dessert. He got up to look at the dessert display and came back and said, "I know what I want. It's this hexagonal torte that's part raspberry mousse and part chocolate." So he ordered that, and it came, and it was a regular, triangular piece of dessert.

And my immediate thought was, *That's not hexagonal. I can never love you. You don't even know basic shapes.*

Then a second thought occurred to me and, pretending that I had to go to the bathroom, I got up and snuck over to the dessert case. Indeed, his dessert was only a slice of an originally hexagonal torte. So I went back to the table, realizing that I could love him after all.

Then he told me he was a heroin addict.

These haiku started as an attempt to prevent all these miserable afternoons and evenings from being a total waste. If I wasn't going to get a soul mate out of them, at the very least I could get some seventeen-syllable poems.

Joel Derfner

P.S.: If I've dated or slept with you and any of these haiku seem to be referring to you, they're not. They're about somebody else. You were divine.

Gay Haiku

I don't understand.
You love it when I do that—
Wait, no. That's Stephen.

Frantically hiding
Porno and Mapplethorpe prints—
Mom is on her way.

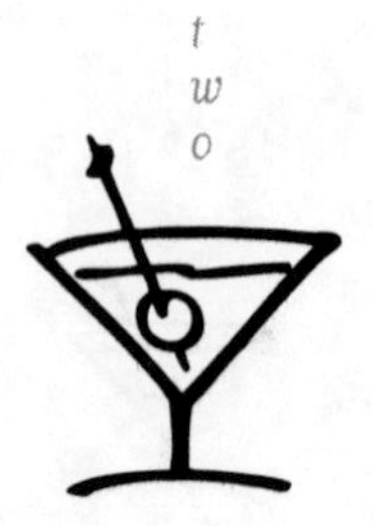

*R*emember when I
Said I disliked oral sex?
I meant just with you.

My seventh birthday;
I weep at Barbie's Dream House.
How could you not know?

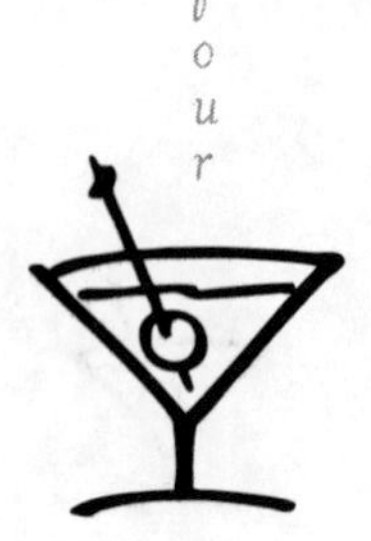

The salmon's divine,
But I'm afraid we can't stay—
I fucked our waiter.

It's our second date,
And I'm not sure I love you.
It's time to break up.

*Y*ou were perfection.
Then you misspelled "embarrassed."
Don't call me again.

He's gorgeous, witty,
And stimulating. Please, God,
Let him be a top.

You fill me with joy
Ineffable, unending.
What's your name again?

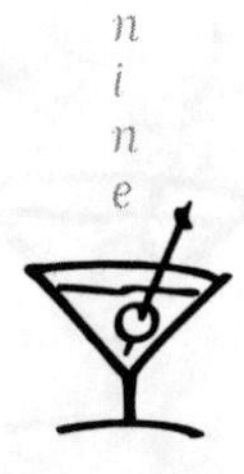

I had a good time—
Hope I'll see you again soon.
(Here, "soon" means "never.")

ten

Gay marriage gives us
The most vital right of all:
Registry at Saks.

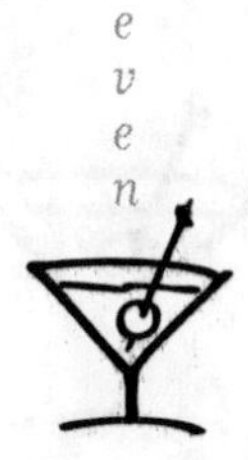

twelve

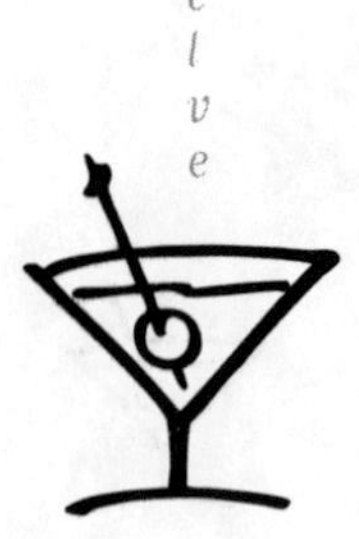

"You understand, right?"

Yes, of course I understand.

And I hope you die.

Dilemma at Pride:
March with the Schubert Lovers
Or the Leather Bears?

thirteen

fourteen

Why is it you fuck
As hard and fast as you can?
I'm not PlayStation.

See the eight-year-old
Knitting mittens on the bus.
Does his mother know?

fifteen

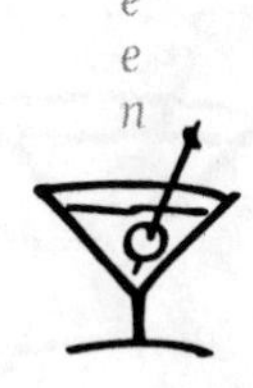

sixteen

Forty-seven times
You said, "Give me that pussy."
I have no pussy.

*T*he romance is gone,
But we're staying together
For the apartment.

seventeen

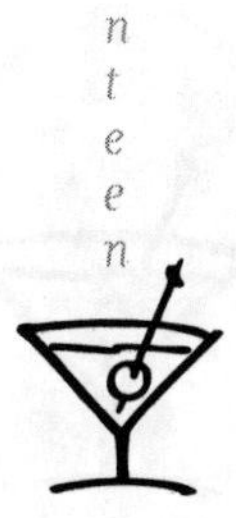

e
i
g
h
t
e
e
n

Yes, I'm a redhead
All over, top to bottom.
Shame you'll never know.

Yes, this feels quite good.
Still, could you pick up the pace?
Golden Girls is on.

nineteen

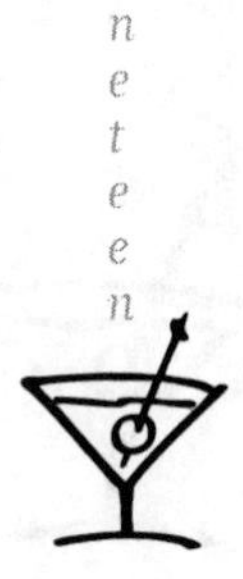

twenty

"Give it to me good—
Oh, yeah, yeah, do it, daddy."
How embarrassing.

See the gay man in
His natural habitat:
Bed Bath & Beyond.

t
w
e
n
t
y

t
w
o

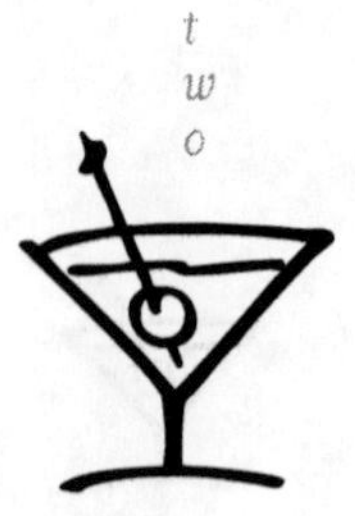

Group sex would be great
If it weren't for this sad truth:
People have elbows.

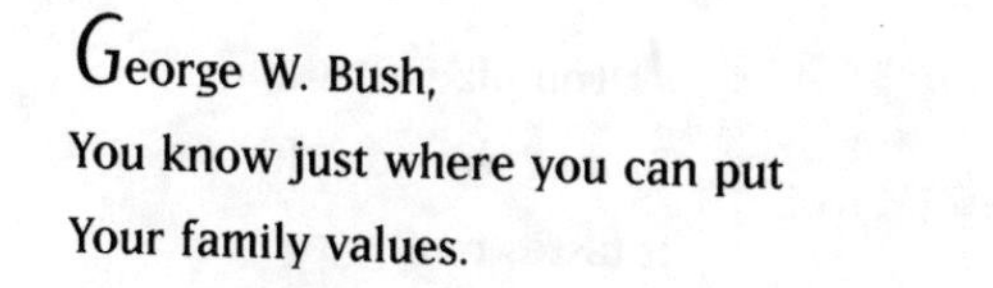

George W. Bush,
You know just where you can put
Your family values.

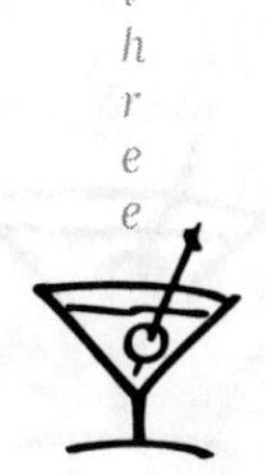

t
w
e
n
t
y

f
o
u
r

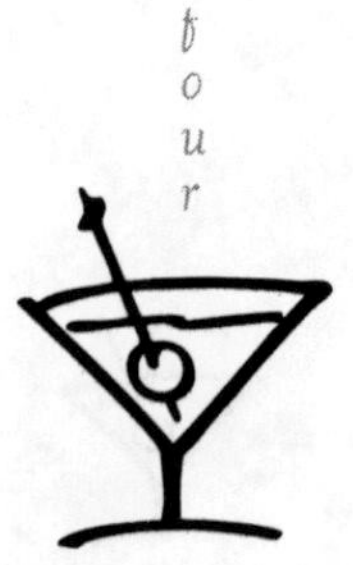

If you plan a tryst,
Do not wear deodorant.
It tastes really gross.

*D*id you just say you
Think *Mansfield Park* is boring?
Get out of my house.

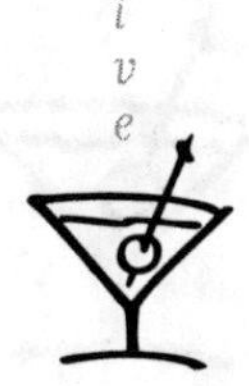

t w e n t y s i x

It's nice to meet you.

Matt said you were a great guy.

So: one dog or two?

Pride: shirtless homos
As far as the eye can see.
My pectorals suck.

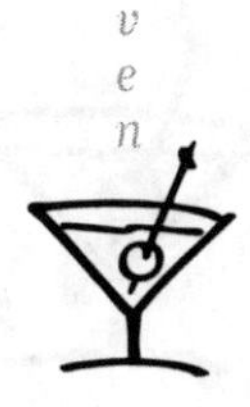

twenty eight

Going mad in Prague: Are all these hot guys gay, or Just European?

"You're a musician?"

"I play skin flute," you answer.

Whoops. There's my cell phone.

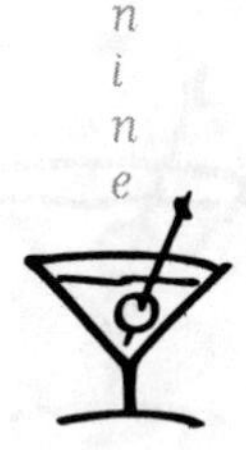

"Let's have a drink first."

Excuse me? I didn't join Men4talk.com.

thirty

At gay synagogue,
Men's heads are bowed deep in prayer.
Why aren't you cruising?

thirty two

The guys screwing on
My TV screen seem so butch.
Then they start to speak.

"*H*ere's *Death in Venice*—
You like murder mysteries."
Should have dumped you then.

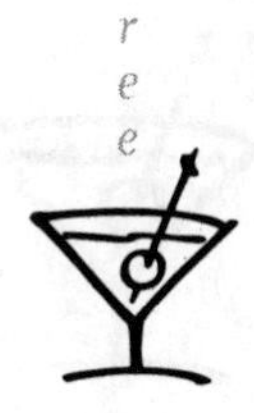

thirty four

Enthralled by the old
Man and the stories he tells:
Gay before Stonewall.

I'm astonishing,

But you still can't get it up.

God, I hate Prozac.

thirty six

How is it you knew
I wasn't faithful? Oh, yeah:
Bite marks on my ass.

You called me "boyfriend"
And I never phoned again.
. . . Thing is, you weren't wrong.

thirty seven

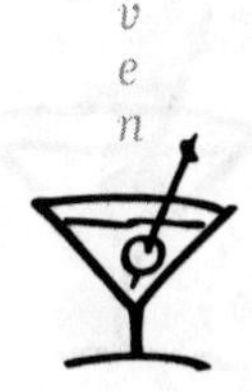

thirty eight

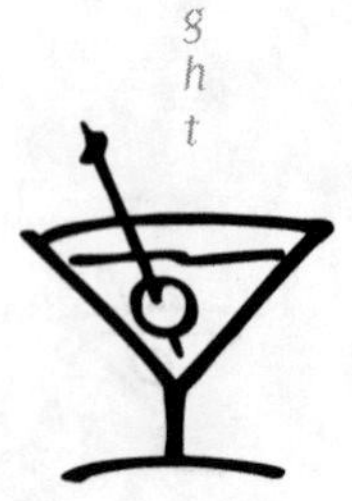

English has no words
For what we just did in bed.
Oh, wait: "Tedious."

Oh, now I get it:
You learned your foreplay technique
From *Powertool 2*.

You're smart and handsome
And rich. Unfortunately,
You live in Jersey.

French kissing is not
A holy, exalted art—
At least not your way.

forty two

"*I* don't understand
Why you want to be with me."
"That's okay. *I* do."

"I need time away,
To figure out who I am."
I can tell you that.

f
o
r
t
y

t
h
r
e
e

forty four

Teens now: out, proud, and
Ignorant of *Auntie Mame.*
Pyrrhic victory?

You have talked and talked
For hours on end. And yet, still,
My watch says 8:10.

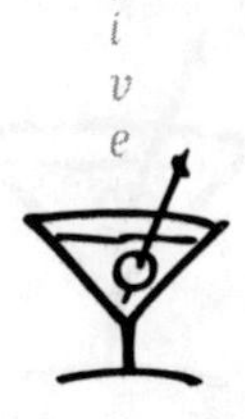

forty six

Headline: "Alien
Loose in New York." That's not news—
I am dating him.

I'm considering
Giving up casual sex:
I hate the subway.

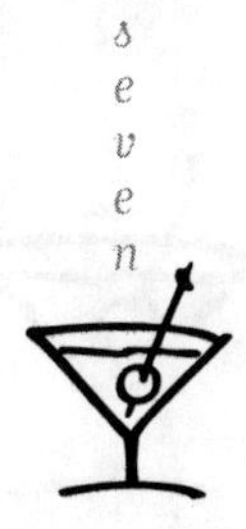

Mother's dilemma:
Her son is gay, but dating
A Jewish doctor.

"*T*his has been fun, but . . ."
I've got news for you, honey:
It wasn't that fun.

forty nine

He's insightful, but—
Could we find a therapist
You haven't slept with?

"Oh, you're on South Beach?
I eat all things and stay thin."
Get out of my sight.

fifty two

I feel so unloved
That I want to kill myself.
It must be Thursday.

Where are all these gays

Going this early? Oh, right:

Sale at Ikea.

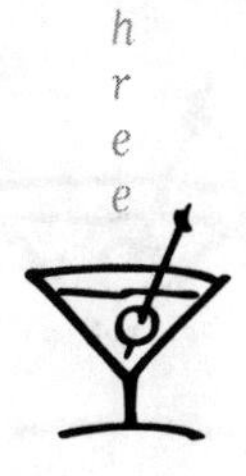

We all make mistakes.
For instance, I mistook you
For a vertebrate.

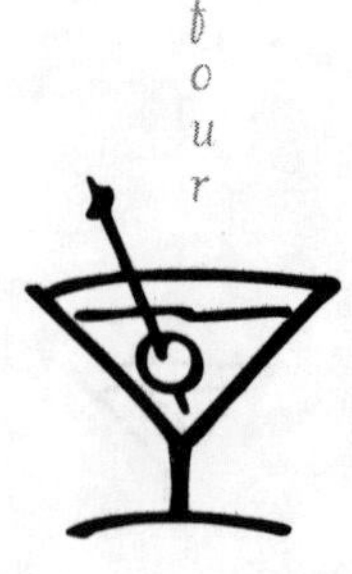

Summer, Cherry Grove:
I gaze, wistful, toward the Pines,
Wishing I were chic.

Your lips are so soft,
Your conversation graceful.
It's just—you're not him.

*W*hen he leaves the room,
If I don't burst into tears,
Then is it still love?

fifty eight

Queer as Folk is trash,
Badly written and acted.
I watch every week.

*B*reak from the orgy:
Stand nude in the kitchen and
Discuss *Top Model.*

*M*an on the subway
Exclaims, "Christ paid your sin bill!"
Christ must be loaded.

You teach aerobics,
Have a physics Ph.D.,
And think my name's Josh.

"I'll call you Wednesday."
The phone didn't ring. Maybe
He meant next Wednesday?

Met a cute ex-gay
Last night. As I suspected,
He was cuter nude.

s
i
x
t
y

f
o
u
r

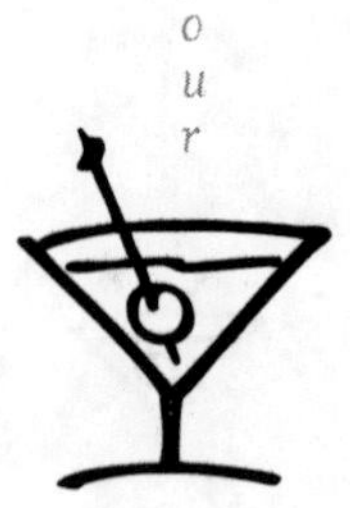

"You're selfish," you said.

"There is no 'i' in 'couple.' "

Not now, there isn't.

Yoga calms my mind.
Then, unfortunately, I
See the teacher's abs.

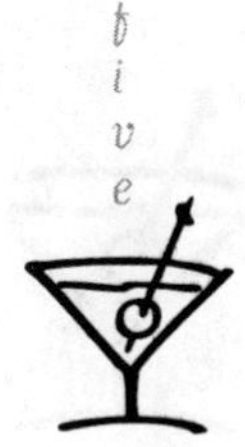

sixty six

My heart is broken.
Maybe he will change his mind
If I lose five pounds?

Your CD rack has
No Barbra, Britney, or Cher.
Are you sure you're gay?

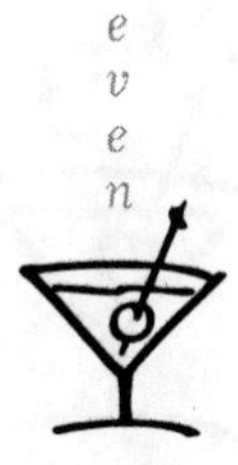

Rule: Kiss toad, get prince.

It's been three weeks. So you can

Change any time now.

I swear I will not
Rest until justice is done:
Vindicate Martha!

sixty nine

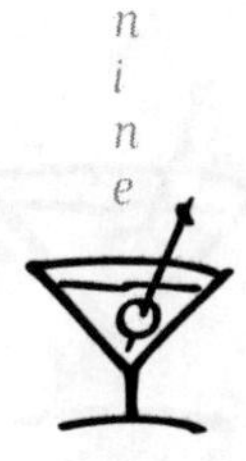

I'm not judgmental.
It's just that I have standards
You will never meet.

Minister Fred Phelps:
Depraved homophobe with a
Really bad hairdo.

seventy two

"The spark is just gone."
I can fix that easy, with
Some gas and a match.

Painting the hall—I
Want blue; you insist on mauve.
Will we make it through?

seventy four

You have updated
Your online dating profile—
At least now I know.

First date; you are a
Log Cabin Republican.
Someone shoot me now.

Lovers at the gym:
Matching A&F tank tops
Make me want to hurl.

You're cruel and petty
And you like to make me cry.
When can you move in?

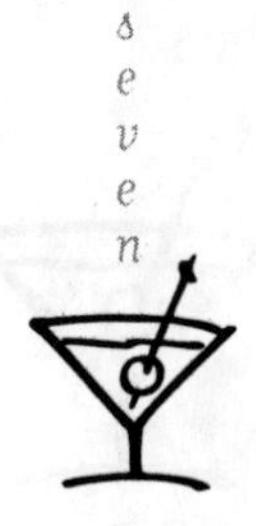

s
e
v
e
n
t
y

e
i
g
h
t

"He has a boyfriend."

"No," you say, "they've broken up."

Paralyzed with hope.

Dinner at your mom's—
I nod, smile, and pretend not
To notice the dust.

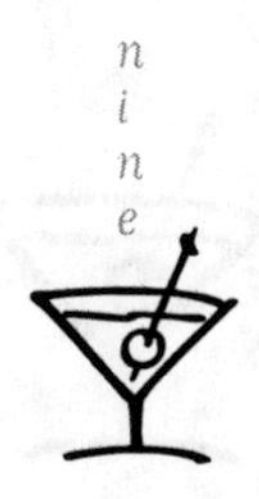

Yes, I forgive you.
I understand—you're human.
Though, on second thought . . .

Walking through Chelsea
Wearing last year's Versace:
I'm a pariah.

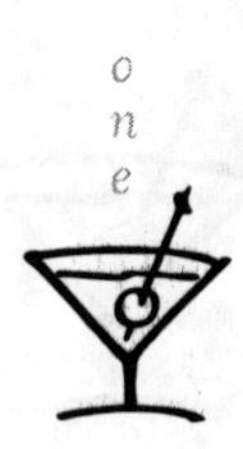

"I'm very flattered,
But, to be honest with you . . ."
Why can't you just lie?

I am giving you
The best shot possible. So:
What's with the poking?

You fill my heart when
I see you. The question is . . .
Is it full enough?

It's Dorian Gray
In reverse: you aged, and yet
Your photo stayed young.

You are judgmental,
Withholding, and cold. Jesus—
I'm dating my mom.

"I have a boyfriend."

We've been talking three hours.

You are a bastard.

eighty eight

My therapist and
All my friends say, "Stay with him!"
They can't hear you snore.

Your room is filled with
Leather and *Star Wars* figures.
Um, I have to go.

Art, music, theater,
Apricot-mango face scrub—
What haven't gays done?

"I'm coming!" you shout,
As if no one had ever
Managed it before.

n
i
n
e
t
y

t
w
o

"Yeah, suck it, big boy."
This is fun, I guess. But I
Could be reading Proust.

We just met—I think
We might be going too fast.
So I won't swallow.

How can we fix us?

The fights, the silence . . . I know!

Let's get a puppy!

As I leave, my clothes
Back on, I realize what's wrong:
Have you got some gel?

You are not the man
I always dreamed I would love—
Just the man I do.

That's not ten inches—
Unless you happen to be
Counting in base 5.

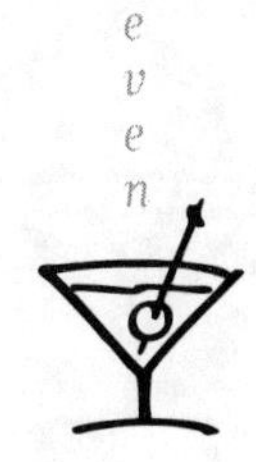

ninety eight

I'm on a new diet:
Atkins for the Soul. Sorry,
But you're full of carbs.

I'd say "I love you"—
But I'm worried that I won't
Mean it tomorrow.

ninety nine

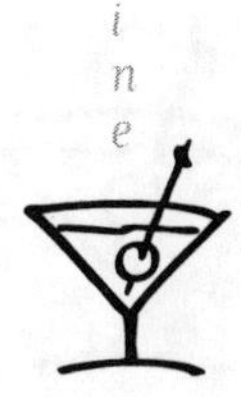

Ab *Fab* preempted
By *Queer Eye for the Straight Guy:*
My life, on TV.

I am over you.
So why, after I see you,
Are my cheeks so wet?

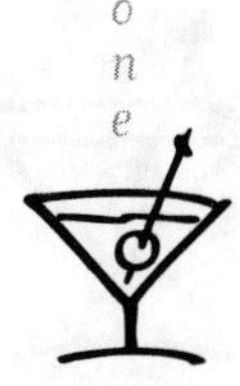

Sitting at the bar,
My soul filled with deep longing
And deeper terror.

This orgy is lame.
But I am, alas, in no
Position to leave.

Summer in P-Town,
Picking up guys left and right:
Thank God for my dog.

No more empty sex:
It is interfering with
My TV schedule.

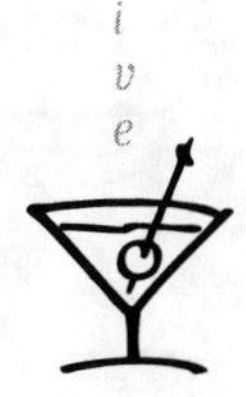

I'm turning thirty:
Today, a birthday party—
Tomorrow, the home.

I know you think I
Like it when you slap my ass.
You are mistaken.

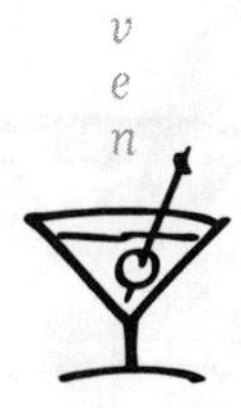

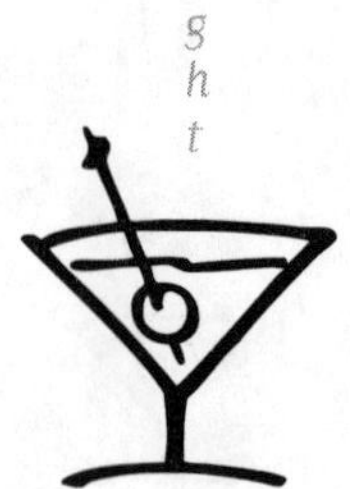

Flailing to the beat—
Could I possibly look half
As dumb as I feel?

Last night, you looked hot.
Today, you want to discuss
The whole foods movement.

"Hope springs eternal."
Don't people realize this is
A very bad thing?

Acknowledgments

I'd like to thank, in (sort of) alphabetical order: Victoria Cain, whose pretense that I wasn't whining should win her an Academy Award; Andrew Corbin, who is the sexiest editor in New York; my father, Armand, whose unconditional support of my every undertaking both mystifies and delights me; my brother, Jeremy, who is the most forbearing roommate in the world, and his girlfriend, Valeri Kiesig, who helped me figure out how to put these things together; Sean Flahaven and Sarah Schlesinger, who unwittingly provided the impetus for this project in the first place; Lisa Halliday, whose first choice

acknowledgments

was indeed the correct one; Rob Hartmann and David Buscher, whose offhand suggestion in a cab gave birth to my career as a professional homosexual; Erika Moore, who has been even more enthusiastic about this project than I; Sarah Rose, whose ability to promote is exceeded only by her ability to write; Len Schiff, Rachel Sheinkin, and Peter Ullian, who are brilliance personified; Andrea Somberg, who is the sexiest agent in New York; Eric Wolff, who has kept me somewhere in the neighborhood of sane; and, last and definitely most, Mike Combs, who seems, bafflingly, to have forgiven me not only for the haiku that are about him but also for the ones that aren't.